The Twirly Skirt

FOR NORA

The TWIRLY SKIRT

by Martha Goldberg

pictures by Helen Stone

WILDSIDE PRESS

Almost Twins

Terry opened her closet door.

Right in front, hung her new party dress. It had lace at the neck and sleeves, a full, full skirt, and a wide sash that tied in the back. She had looked at it at least six times today. She could hardly wait to wear it on her birthday next Saturday.

The doorbell buzzed.

Terry closed the closet door slowly. Then she ran to answer the bell because her mother was out doing the Saturday marketing.

There stood her friend Jean jingling her skates. "Hi, get your skates and come on out."

"Come on in first," Terry said. "I want to show you something."

She led Jean to her room and threw open the closet door.

"Oo-h!" cried Jean, "a yellow party dress!"

"My birthday present."

"Yellow's my favorite color," Jean said.

"It's mine, too."

Terry lifted out the dress on the hanger and gave it a quick twist. As it twirled around, the full skirt flew out with a swish.

"Oh, Terry! it's got a twirly skirt!" Jean touched the stiff silk. "A dress with a twirly skirt is just what I want," she added.

"Can't you get one for your birthday present, too?" Terry asked.

"Oh maybe I could!" Jean said with joy.

"Then you could wear it to *your* birthday party."

6

Jean's smile faded. "What's the use? I can't have a party anyhow."

"You can't?" Terry cried.

Jean shook her head sadly. "My mother told me this morning that she has to work in the store every Saturday from now on. She can't even get the Saturday of my birthday off."

Now Terry felt sad. For weeks they had planned their birthday parties, hers next Saturday and Jean's the Saturday after. And they were *both* going to be eight.

Why, Terry thought, we're the same age, and we live on the same street, and we go to the same school. Jean is my best friend and I am hers. We do everything together.

That's it! Together! It's so simple.

"Jean, you can have your party with me next Saturday!"

"Will your mother let me?"

"Sure she will. I'll ask her."

"And I'll ask my Mom. Her bus will get here any time now." Jean's whole face lighted up. "Oh, Terry, we'll be just like twins!"

Terry was still holding her dress. Jean reached out and took the hanger from her. Then she twirled the dress around. The skirt flew out "swish" in a wide circle.

"Why don't you try it on?" Terry asked.

"Oh! I'd like to!" Jean cried. "But we've got to go meet that bus now."

She quickly hung the dress in the closet. Terry picked up her skates, and they ran outside.

They saw Jean's mother getting off the bus and skated toward her so fast that they were puffing for breath when they reached her.

Jean grabbed her mother's arm to keep her-

9

self from falling. "A twin party, Mom!" she cried.

And Terry asked in a rush, "Can Jean have her birthday with me?"

"What's all this about?" Jean's mother asked.

So they told her their idea for a party together.

She smiled at their excitement. "I'll have to ask Terry's mother. After all, she'll be doing most of the work. I'll phone her," she said. "And I'll bake the birthday cakes. You both can help me."

She started walking toward home and Terry and Jean skated along beside her.

"Mom," Jean asked, "now can I have a party dress for my birthday present, a twin dress like Terry's?"

"Why, honey, your pink dress looks lovely on you."

"But Mom," Jean cried excitedly, "the last time I wore that old dress the sleeve tore. You said you couldn't mend it because it was so tight it would only tear again."

"Yes, I remember now. I'd get you a new dress if I could take you shopping." Her mother looked worried.

Jean stopped skating and turned her face away.

Her mother put an arm around her. "Look, dear, I'll try to get the time off. But I can't promise."

Jean pulled away from her mother's arm and skated

12

ahead slowly. Then she called over her shoulder in a loud voice, "Oh I don't care! I really didn't want a new dress anyway!" She skated quickly away, leaving her mother and Terry behind.

But Jean does care, Terry thought. She *said* she wanted a dress like mine. She even wanted to try mine on.

Terry turned to Jean's mother. "My Mom ought to be home by now. I'll go ask her about the twin party. Bye."

And she skated on home, wondering if there was any way that Jean could get a new dress.

13

TERRY burst into the
kitchen and dropped her
skates. They clattered on
the floor.

Her mother was sitting
at the table slicing apples.

"Mom, can Jean have her birthday party

with me? Her mother has to work every Saturday, so she can't give her a party. Say 'yes', Mom, please."

"Why, yes, of course," her mother said, and went on slicing apples.

Terry threw herself on her mother and gave her a hug.

"Look out for the knife!"

Terry stepped back. Then she said, "Jean's mother will bake the birthday cakes. She's going to phone you. Mm-yum, apple pie," Terry added, and took a slice of apple.

"Don't take the slices for the pie. Get an apple and cut it up yourself."

Her mother's voice seemed to come from far away. Terry was only half listening because she was wondering how Jean could get a dress. She reached for another piece of apple.

"Now really, Terry, if you want a pie leave these slices alone."

"I'm sorry, Mom, but I was thinking about Jean's dress."

"What dress?"

"A party dress like mine, but her mother can't take her shopping, and it won't seem like a real birthday for Jean if she hasn't a new dress. She wants one so badly. She ought to have a twin dress like mine, Mom, we're almost —!"

The words were tumbling out, but suddenly Terry stopped talking. Almost twins—

why if they were real twin sisters, they'd go shopping together!

She shouted excitedly, "Mom, *we* could take Jean shopping!"

"Why yes, I suppose we could," her mother answered.

"Boy! I'm going to call her right now."

After Terry talked to Jean the two mothers talked together. Terry heard hers say, "I can take them to town Tuesday."

Now Jean is going to have her party and her new dress, too! Terry thought happily.

A Dress for Jean

Tuesday after school Jean and Terry and her mother all went to Tinkles, the store where Terry had bought her dress.

In the girls' department, rows of dresses hung on a long rack. Terry's mother sat down to wait for a clerk, but the two girls ran to the rack. There Terry spied a yellow dress.

"Here's one with a twirly skirt–like mine!"

The clerk who had sold Terry her dress

came over to them and asked, "Would you
like to try it on?"

"*I* would!" Jean said.

She took off her own dress and quickly
slipped the yellow one on. Before anyone
could button it or tie the sash she twirled
across the floor to the mirror.

Terry watched her spin round and round.
There were two Jeans—one in the mirror and

one in front of it. Both with flying curls and yellow dresses that spun out in a circle. Jean was twins!

"Come here, dear," Terry's mother called, "and let me see how it fits."

"Oh I know it fits," Jean said as she walked back. "Please, let's buy it."

"But the dress is tight across the shoulders, dear, and quite short. You'd grow out of it before long."

A Dress for Jean

Jean hung her head. She looked ready to cry.

Terry pushed the row of dresses along the rack. "Isn't there a larger one?" she asked.

The clerk went to the back of the store to look. Then she brought out two yellow dresses but not a yellow one that was like Terry's.

"I haven't that one any larger," the clerk said, "but you can try these on."

"They're not the same," Jean said. "They haven't even got twirly skirts."

Terry wondered what they would do now. She looked at her mother.

Her mother looked at the clerk, and asked, "Can't you order the one she wants in a larger size?"

The clerk went to the desk and telephoned.

The girls waited anxiously. What if she couldn't find another twirly skirt!

But the clerk came back smiling. "They have your size in our other store."

Jean sighed, too glad to speak. She took Terry's hand.

Terry danced her around. She thought she would burst with happiness.

"Let's go get it now," Jean begged in an eager voice.

"The other store will be closed before we could get there," Terry's mother answered. "The clerk can send it."

"Tomorrow?" Jean and Terry both spoke together.

"No, Thursday afternoon is the next delivery," said the clerk. "Where shall I send it?"

22

A Dress for Jean

Jean sighed, and gave her address.

Then they went upstairs to the toy department to buy the party things.

"Let's have everything yellow to match our yellow dresses," Terry said.

"And some green things, too," Jean said.

So they chose a laughing clown dressed in

yellow and green for the center of the table. They bought a yellow paper tablecloth and napkins to match. They bought green paper plates and nut cups like clown faces, and funny clown hats. They bought small parasols and bright colored balloons, and green candles for the birthday cakes. Then they went to a candy store and chose hard candies and peanuts to put in the nut cups.

Now all they had to do was invite their friends to the twin party.

Hundreds of Delivery Trucks

It was a long wait until Thursday afternoon. At last it came, and school was out. The two girls rushed home to Jean's.

They found a folded paper pushed part way under the door.

Jean pulled it out and began to read. Terry looked over her shoulder and read, too.

25

"Oh no!" she cried.

For the paper said that the delivery man from Tinkles had been there with the dress and no one had been home.

So the twirly skirt had gone back to the store again.

Two big tears rolled down Jean's cheeks.

"We should have had them send it to my house," Terry said. "My mother is most always home."

They sat down on the steps.

Jean twisted a button on her sweater. Terry pushed her toe

round and round on the step. Even if they went to the store the dress would not be there. The delivery man still had it in his truck.

"Maybe my mother will phone the store and have them send it to our house." Terry said, jumping up and pulling Jean to her feet. "Come on."

Terry's mother did telephone Tinkles, and the clerk told her that the dress would be sent out again Saturday morning.

Jean skipped around the room happily.

But Terry was worried. Saturday morning! The day of the party! Suppose the dress did not come in time? Suppose the delivery man took it to Jean's house again and no one was there?

That night she forgot to worry. They had

27

so much fun helping Jean's mother make the birthday cakes.

Terry beat the eggs until they were fluffy. Jean creamed the butter and sugar.

While the cakes were baking Jean's mother made the frosting and colored one part yellow and the other part green. When the cakes were done and had cooled, she spread them with the yellow frosting. Then, with green frosting, she wrote "Happy Birthday Terry" on one and "Happy Birthday Jean" on the other.

Terry and Jean put a row of candy flowers around each cake. Then they scraped the frosting pans and licked the spoons.

Later, when Terry was asleep, she dreamed that hundreds of delivery trucks drove down

her street and brought thousands of boxes to
her. She piled them in every room of her
house. More and more boxes kept coming
and Terry opened them all. She was trying
to find Jean's dress with the twirly skirt in
time for the party.

Hundreds of Delivery Trucks

SATURDAY morning it seemed that half the delivery trucks in town came down Terry's street. But none were from Tinkles. Twice the doorbell rang. Once it was the laundryman and the next time it was a man selling brushes.

Then the doorbell rang again. Surely this time it was Tinkles. But it wasn't.

Jean herself skipped in. "Where's my dress?" she asked with a big smile.

"It hasn't come yet," Terry said.

The smile left Jean's face.

"But it will come; they promised," Terry added quickly. "Come on, let's get things ready for the party while we're waiting."

They spread the paper tablecloth on the

table and set the laughing clown in the center. They put the funny clown hats, and the plates and napkins and nut cups at each place. Then they walked around the table and filled the nut cups with peanuts and hard candies.

A car stopped outside. Jean ran to the front window, but she came back shaking her head. "It's not Tinkles—only the milkman."

They wrapped the parasols in yellow paper and tied them with green ribbon bows and set one a each place. Then they tied the balloons to the backs of the chairs.

"Boy!" Terry stepped back to look at the finished table.

Then she turned to Jean. "Let's get the things for the games now. Your dress is sure to come soon."

The Twirly Skirt

They set up a card table in the living room. On it they put a jar of beans, a tin pie plate, two potatoes, a handkerchief, and ten paper donkey tails with pins pushed through them. They fastened a large donkey picture to the wall near the card table.

Still the dress had not come. So they went into the kitchen and each put eight green candles on her own cake.

Terry's mother gave them lunch. Terry ate a small sandwich and drank a glass of milk, but Jean did not feel like finishing hers.

"Do you think they forgot to send my dress?" she asked Terry's mother anxiously.

"No, I don't," she answered. "But it's nearly time to dress."

"I guess I'll have to go home and put on

my old party dress," Jean said. She walked out the door, holding back the tears.

"That old Tinkles!" Terry cried. She stamped into her own room. She did not feel as glad as she thought she would about putting on her new dress. She took it from the closet and held it under her chin. It really was beautiful.

Then, still holding the dress before her, she danced around the room. The dress danced with her. It twisted and twirled as she turned and made a low rustlely sound. When she stopped before the mirror the skirt fell into stiff folds. When she turned around again it opened out wide.

She stopped and slipped the dress on over her head. Then she reached back to fasten it, but her fingers could not find the small buttons. Her mother would have to do it.

"Oh my yellow yellow tw-wirl-ly skirt," Terry sang. She spun out of her room toward the kitchen.

She stopped in the dining room to look at the yellow and green party table. Everything was set for the party. No, not everything, she remembered. Jean hasn't her new dress and has gone home to put on her old one.

How could she, Terry, wear her new dress? But she wanted to wear it! Why, she had gotten it specially for her birthday! But then, this was going to be a twin party, hers and Jean's. It would seem mostly hers, if she wore a new dress and Jean didn't. How could she? No, she just couldn't!

If Jean had to wear her old party dress, she would wear her old one, too.

Terry walked slowly back to her room. "That old Tinkles!" she cried again. "It's spoiled the party!" She slammed the door hard.

Two Cakes

Terry had just changed when Jean came back.

"You didn't put on your twirly skirt!" Jean cried.

"I-couldn't." Terry looked down at her own dress then across at Jean's.

Jean tried to smile. "Anyhow, we're almost twins. We both have old dresses on."

The sharp ring of the doorbell made Terry jump.

"Your dress!" she shouted to Jean.

But outside the door stood their friends Doris and Cindy. Peggy and her mother, who was to help with the party, were behind them, and down the street they could see Jane and Kay, and Pam and Linda, and Betsy, too.

"Hi," Terry and Jean called together.

"Happy birthday! Happy birthday!" everyone shouted as they ran up and went into the house.

The Twirly Skirt

First they had a potato race. Then they played spin the plate, and a bean guessing game.

Then they took turns pinning tails on the donkey. Doris had just pinned a tail on and Jane was taking the handkerchief from her eyes when the doorbell rang again.

Terry dashed to the door.

There stood a man with a large box. "Package from Tinkles," he said.

Terry grabbed it and gave it to Jean, shouting, "It came! It really, really came!"

Jean knelt on the floor and quickly tore off the cover of the box. Then slowly she lifted the dress from its paper wrappings. She held the swishy yellow skirt against herself.

"Look! It's just right!" she cried.

"Put it on," Cindy cried. She unbuttoned Jean's old party dress. It slipped to the floor.

Terry lifted the new dress over Jean's head. Jean put her arms up and wiggled and wiggled to make the dress slide down.

Then Terry buttoned it and Cindy tied the sash.

"Oo-ooh, a twirly skirt," the other girls were saying.

Jean did not say a word. Her eyes were on her dress. Her fingers were smoothing the stiff skirt.

Then she began to turn, slowly at first, then faster and faster. Her arms went out, then up and up, and the twirly skirt flew out with a soft "swish."

Jean looked at her friends gathered round.

Her dark eyes sparkled and her long curls bobbed as she twirled in a yellow circle.

"Hi, old spinner!" Terry called.

Jean stopped twirling suddenly. "Terry! Where's your dress?"

"My dress!" Terry shrieked. She had forgotten it!

She began pulling her old dress off and dashed to her room. Jean ran after her.

After them ran the other girls.

Terry took her yellow dress from the closet and quickly put it on.

"Golly, another twirly skirt," Jane cried.

Jean buttoned it and tied the sash.

Then Terry and Jean twirled out of the bedroom and into the dining room. Everyone followed them.

44

The two mothers stood in the doorway. Each one held a lighted birthday cake.

Cindy started singing, "Happy birthday to you, happy birthday to you,—."

Then everyone began to sing and walked with Terry and Jean to the table.

Terry sat down at one end of the table. Her mother set her birthday cake in front of her. Jean sat down at the other end and Peggy's mother set her cake in front of her.

Then they all sang "Happy Birthday" again. This time it was for Jean.

Two Cakes

As the song ended Jean called to Terry, "Let's blow our candles out and make our wishes together!"

So each took a long deep breath. Then with a great puff each blew out all eight candles on her own cake.

"We'll get our wishes," Jean said happily.

Terry looked down the table at Jean in her new yellow dress. "But I've got *my* wish already!" she cried.

Made in the USA
Middletown, DE
02 September 2018